To my daughter Alexandra, and to Chris, Max, and Charlie—with love always. —K. H.
To John and Pauline Craig —H. C.

LITTLE SIMON
An imprint of Simon & Schuster Children's Publishing Division
1230 Avenue of the Americas, New York, New York 10020
First Little Simon hardcover edition August 2021
© 2021 Helen Craig Ltd. and Katharine Holabird.
The Angelina Ballerina name and character and the dancing Angelina logo are trademarks
of HIT Entertainment Limited, Katharine Holabird, and Helen Craig.
All rights reserved, including the right of reproduction in whole or in part in any form.
LITTLE SIMON is a registered trademark of Simon & Schuster, Inc., and associated colophon
is a trademark of Simon & Schuster, Inc.
For information about special discounts for bulk purchases, please contact Simon & Schuster Special Sales
at 1-866-506-1949 or business@simonandschuster.com.
The Simon & Schuster Speakers Bureau can bring authors to your live event. For more information or to book an event
contact the Simon & Schuster Speakers Bureau at 1-866-248-3049 or visit our website at www.simonspeakers.com.
Manufactured in China 0621 SCP
2 4 6 8 10 9 7 5 3 1
ISBN 978-1-5344-9527-2
ISBN 978-1-5344-9528-9 (eBook)

Angelina™ and Alice

Story by **Katharine Holabird** Illustrations by **Helen Craig**

LITTLE SIMON

New York   London   Toronto   Sydney   New Delhi

Angelina jumped for joy the day Alice came to school. Alice loved to dance and do gymnastics, and she was good at all the same things as Angelina. They quickly became close friends and were always together. At breaks they skipped rope and did cartwheels round and round the playground.

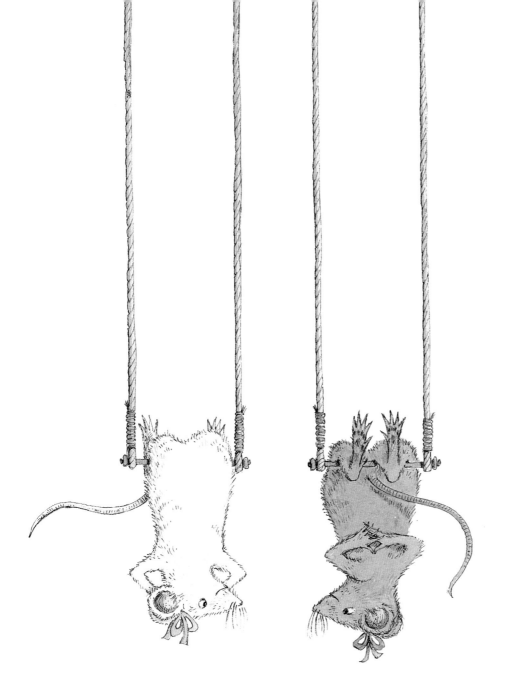

They loved to see who could hang upside down longest on the trapeze bar without wiggling, swing highest on the swings, or do the most somersaults in the air.

Angelina was good at cartwheels and could even do the splits, but Alice could do a perfect handstand with her toes pointed straight in the air and never lose her balance.

Angelina always fell over when she tried to do a handstand, which was embarrassing, especially on the playground.

One day Angelina fell right on her bottom, and the older children pointed at her and laughed. One of them giggled and said, "Look at Angelina Tumbelina!" Another whispered to Alice, and then...

. . .something awful happened. Alice giggled too, and ran off to play with the older children while Angelina sat behind the swings and cried.

The next day was worse. All the children said, "Angelina Tumbelina!" on the playground, and Angelina couldn't find Alice anywhere. Angelina couldn't concentrate at school and made lots of mistakes in her spelling. She couldn't eat her sandwiches at lunch either, and by the time the class was lining up for gym, Angelina felt so sick that she wished she could go home.

Mr. Hopper, the gym teacher, blew his whistle for silence and said, "You've all worked so hard at your gymnastics over the year that we are going to do a show for the village festival. Everyone needs to find a partner and start practicing now."

Angelina looked at the floor. Who could she ask? She was afraid nobody would be her partner. A big tear rolled down her nose.

Then she felt a tap on her shoulder. It was Alice!
"Will you be my partner, please?" Alice asked.

All that afternoon Angelina and
Alice worked on handstands in the
gymnasium. "Just keep your head
down and line up your tail with the
tip of your nose," Alice said patiently.
"That always helps me to stay up
straight longer." Alice was a good
teacher, and soon Angelina could do
a handstand without falling at all.

Mr. Hopper taught them how to swing in a beautiful circle over the bar and how to actually fly through the air and land neatly balanced on the mat.

He taught them to work with the rings and on the bars

and to do rhythmic gymnastics with colored ribbons.

Finally, Mr. Hopper showed them
a terrific balancing trick they could
do for the show.

The day of the village festival was
bright and beautiful.

TODAY
A DISPLAY
OF
GYMNASTICS
BY THE
CHILDREN
OF
MOUSELING
School.

The gymnastics class did a wonderful display at the village festival with high jumps, backflips, and balancing on the bars. When Angelina and Alice did their balancing act together, even the older children were impressed. "Wow!" they said. "How did you learn to do those amazing tricks?"

PIN THE TAIL ON THE CAT & WIN A PRIZE!

After the show Mr. Hopper smiled and said, "That was really good teamwork!"

Alice and Angelina grinned back. "That's because we're such good friends," they said together.